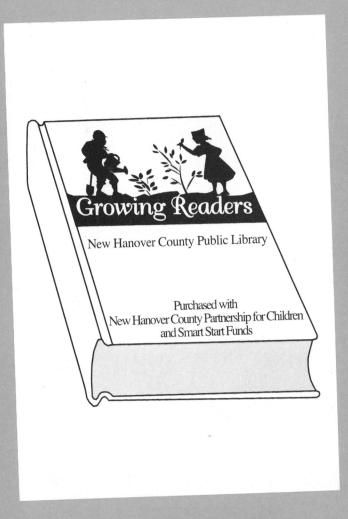

Homemade LOVE

bell hooks

with pictures by
Shane W. Evans

JUMP AT THE SUN
HYPERION BOOKS FOR CHILDREN
NEW YORK

Text copyright © 2002 by bell hooks
Illustrations copyright © 2002 by Shane W. Evans
All rights reserved. No part of this book may be reproduced or transmitted
in any form or by any means, electronic or mechanical, including photocopying,
recording, or by any information storage and retrieval system,
without written permission from the publisher. For information address
Hyperion Books for Children, 114 Fifth Avenue, New York, New York 10011-5690.

First Edition
1 3 5 7 9 10 8 6 4 2
Printed in Singapore
This book is set in Filosofia.
Book design by Polly Kanevsky
Visit www.jumpatthesun.com

Library of Congress Cataloging-in-Publication Data
hooks, bell.
Homemade love / by bell hooks;
pictures by Shane W. Evans.—1st ed.
p.   cm.
Summary: Through the constant love
and support of her parents,
Girlpie learns not to be afraid of the dark.
ISBN 0-7868-0643-5
(1. Love—Fiction. 2. Family life—Fiction.
3. Afro-Americans—Fiction.) I. Evans, Shane W., ill. II. Title.
PZ7.H7663 Ho 2002
(E)—dc21
99-59839

home making,
home cooking,
you created a world of taste
and flavors
good food, good times
sustained pleasure
for you, mama—Rosa Bell

all good good!

—b.h.

Thank you, God.
Dedicated to the
original Girlpie, Renee

—S.W.E.

My mama calls me girlpie.

Her
Sweet

sweet.

Daddy's
honey bun
chocolate
Dew Drop.

Love.

All good

good

good.

But everything I do
cannot be right.
'Cause there is no
ALL
THE
TIME
RIGHT.

But all the time
    any hurt can be healed.
All wrongs forgiven.
    And all the
world made

Peace again.

Let Life go on.

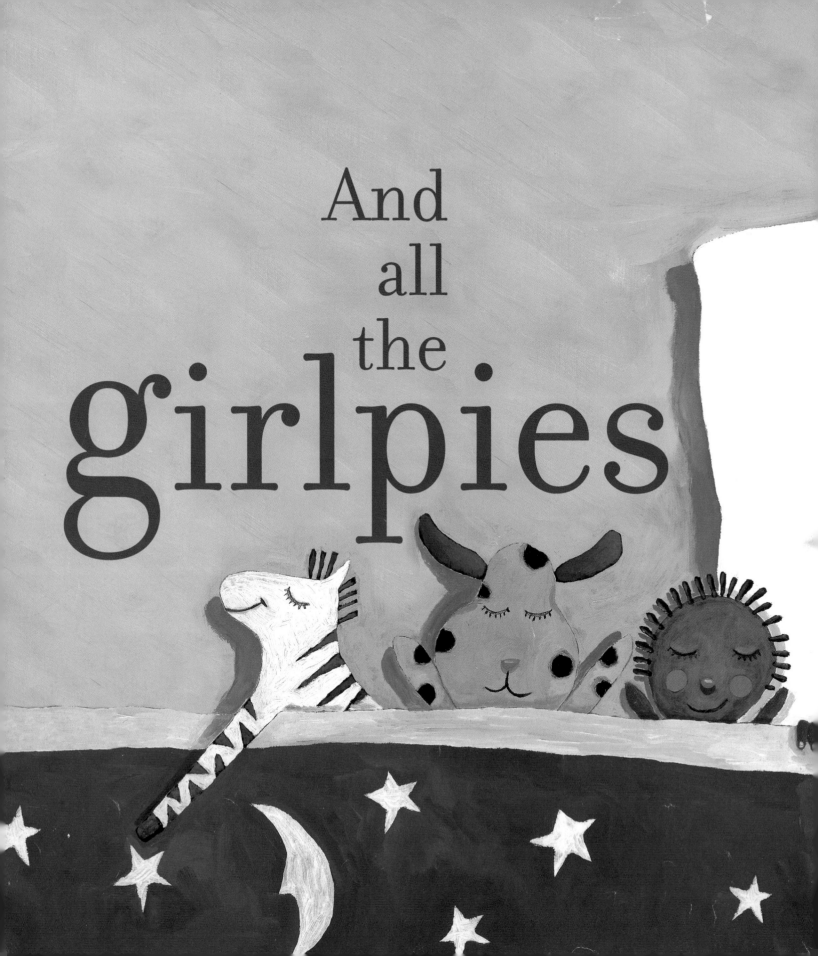

And all the girlpies

sleep
tenderly.

Lost in
deep
dreams.
Nighttime
surrender.

Closed
door
sleep
alone
time.

Memories
of arms
that
hold me

holding me still.

No need
to fear the
dark place.

'Cause
everywhere
is

Home.